The Lady with the Books

A Story Inspired by the Remarkable Work of Jella Lepman

Kathy Stinson **Marie Lafrance**

Kids Can Press

To the late Jella Lepman, whose work has enriched the lives of children around the world for generations — K.S.

To my father, who gave me the best gift of my first books and went on to feed me classics and historical novels, whether I wanted them or not — M.L.

Acknowledgments

I owe thanks for this book to a great number of people. They know why. Katie Scott, Yvette Ghione and Marie Bartholomew at Kids Can Press; Marie Lafrance; Miriam Koërner; Peter Carver; Nan Forler; Heather Smith; Donna Grassby; Lena Coakley; Paula Wing; Hadley Dyer; Sabine Brandtl at Haus der Kunst; Karl Stankiewitz; Christine Hannig at the Monacensia; Nadine Zimmermann at the International Youth Library; Binette and Peter Schroeder; Susanne Kohlbeck at the Bavarian State Library; Gian-Luca Pia at the Hotel Blutenburg; and the Ontario Arts Council.

Author's Note

Winnie-the-Pooh by A. A. Milne was first published in English in 1926. It was one of the books in Jella Lepman's traveling exhibition but was not translated into German, as *Pu der Bär*, until 1947. The author has exercised artistic license in having Anneliese remember Papa reading that book to her in order to give her a reading experience that many contemporary readers, reading in many languages, will relate to.

The German words in the story are:
danke (DAHN-kuh): thank you
oma (OO-mah): grandmother
Pu der Bär (POO derh BEAR): *Winnie-the-Pooh*
wurst (VOORST): sausage

Photo Credits: Jella Lepman (page 28): © Stiftung Internationale Jugendbibliothek, Poehlmann. Haus der Kunst exhibition, 1946 (page 30) and International Youth Library (page 31): © Stiftung Internationale Jugendbibliothek. *The Story of Ferdinand* book cover (page 29): Courtesy of Penguin Random House LLC. *Histoire de Babar* book cover (page 29): Courtesy of L'école des loisirs.

Kids Can Press gratefully acknowledges the financial support of the Government of Ontario, through Ontario Creates; the Ontario Arts Council; the Canada Council for the Arts; and the Government of Canada for our publishing activity.

Published in Canada and the U.S. by Kids Can Press Ltd.

25 Dockside Drive, Toronto, ON M5A 0B5

Kids Can Press is a Corus Entertainment Inc. company

www.kidscanpress.com

The artwork in this book was rendered in graphite pencil and colored digitally in Photoshop.

The text is set in Bauer bodoni.

Edited by Katie Scott
Designed by Marie Bartholomew

Printed and bound in Buji, Shenzhen, China, in 03/2020 by WKT Company

CM 20 0 9 8 7 6 5 4 3 2 1

Library and Archives Canada Cataloguing in Publication

Title: The lady with the books : a story inspired by the remarkable work of Jella Lepman / Kathy Stinson ; illustrations by Marie Lafrance.
Names: Stinson, Kathy, author. | Lafrance, Marie, illustrator.
Identifiers: Canadiana 20190208996 | ISBN 9781525301544 (hardcover)
Subjects: LCSH: Lepman, Jella — Juvenile fiction.
Classification: LCC PS8587.T56 L33 2020 | DDC jC813/.54 — dc23

“Let us set this upside-down world right again by starting with the children. They will show the grown-ups the way to go.”

— Jella Lepman, 1945

FREE SOUP

Anneliese kicked at the dirt and rubble on the sidewalk. Women were still clearing away chunks of broken buildings and pavement with brooms and their bare hands. Couldn't they see that the street would never be what it had been before the war?

At the market, Anneliese spotted an orange peel on the ground. She wiped off the dirt as best she could, and even though her stomach grumbled, she gave it to her brother.

Peter gnawed the inside of it. "Mmm," he said. "*Danke.*"

Nearby, a line of people was disappearing into a long building.

Maybe, Anneliese thought, someone was giving out food. She took Peter's hand and moved into the line.

Inside the great hall were books! More books than Anneliese could count! She felt her heart lift, then a sudden pang.

Papa used to take her to the library. When he read her *Pu der Bär* at bedtime, he used a different voice for every character: the donkey, the kangaroo, the piglet and, best of all, Pu himself.

Now the library was gone. And Papa was gone, too.

Across the room, a lady was pulling books from a shelf and talking excitedly to a group of adults. Anneliese caught the word *hope* just as Peter began tugging on her sleeve.

"Read me this?"

"I can't read that language," Anneliese said. "Why do you want a story about an elephant anyway?"

"Because I've never seen an elephant in a suit before!"

Anneliese and Peter got so busy looking at books they didn't notice when they were the only visitors left in the hall. The lady with the books came over and said, "I'm afraid the exhibition is closing now."

Peter hugged the elephant book to his chest. "May I please take this home?"

"I'm sorry," the lady said. "I wish you could. But you are welcome to come back tomorrow."

Out on the street, Peter was too tired to walk. Anneliese picked him up and carried him home.

Mama was cooking up the last of the barley. She gave what little there was to Anneliese and Peter.

After supper, Mama took her *oma's* old teapot from a shelf. It had survived the bombing with just one dent. "Tomorrow," she said, "I'll try to trade it for some fresh vegetables, and maybe a spoonful of butter."

At the market the next day, Anneliese eyed sausages hanging above baskets of fruits and vegetables. Did she dare snatch just one juicy fat *wurst* when the vendor turned his back?

"Can we go back to the book building today?"

Peter's question so surprised Anneliese that she missed her chance. Just as well. Mama wouldn't like it if she'd been caught stealing. And it would be good to be among those books again.

Back inside the great hall, a group of children was gathering around the lady with the books. Peter pulled Anneliese to the front.

"This is *The Story of Ferdinand*," the lady said. "It was written in English, so I'll translate parts of it into German for you. The pictures will help tell the story, too."

As the story unfolded, Peter whispered, "That bull is just like me. He likes flowers, and he doesn't like fighting."

When it was clear that the bull would not fight like the bullfighters wanted him to, Anneliese was afraid to look. Her papa had been shot for standing up to men whose orders he didn't want to follow.

With the turning of the page, Peter started clapping. Anneliese was happy, too, to see Ferdinand — after all he had been through — back on his flowery hill.

"Did you enjoy that?" the lady asked. "Did you have a favorite part?"

"When he wouldn't fight!"

"When he got to go back home."

"When he sat on the bee!"

The lady laughed. "I liked those parts, too."

"Here are more stories I hope you will get to read in German someday: Pinocchio from Italy, Heidi from Switzerland, Babar from France."

"That's my elephant!" said Peter.

Turning to Anneliese, the lady said, "I think you would like this story from Sweden. Pippi has no parents, and when the police try to take her to an orphanage, she outwits them. She is very clever and very strong. She can lift her pet horse with one hand."

Anneliese smiled. "She has a pet horse?"

"And a pet monkey!"

On the way home, Anneliese thought about Pippi, who had lost both her parents and yet did just fine for herself.

Back home, Mama was poking a long spoon into a pot. Anneliese's mouth watered. "That smells wonderful."

"The farmer was generous," Mama said, "and on the way home, I caught a pigeon. We'll have enough stew for two days!"

That night at bedtime, Peter asked Anneliese for a story.

"Once upon a time," she said, as her brother nestled in beside her, "there was a boy who had a green suit. He liked flowers more than anything. And he had a pet —"

"Horse!" Peter said.

"You'd like a pet horse?"

"Yes. And maybe a monkey."

Later that night, Anneliese awoke. High in the dark sky the moon shone brightly. Careful not to disturb Peter or Mama, she got up and stepped outside.

How beautiful the trees looked in the moonlight. The flowers, too, blooming among the chunks of rubble.

Tomorrow, Anneliese decided, she would join the women with their brooms. She would help clear the street around the damaged library. And maybe someday, the building would again be filled with books.

But for now, she would go back to bed and sleep, like Ferdinand in his field of flowers, and she would dream.

THE LADY WITH THE BOOKS

The lady with the books was a real person.

Jella (pronounced YELL-ah) Lepman was born in Germany in 1891. In 1936, she and her two children had to flee the country. With Adolf Hitler as leader, their lives were in danger because they were Jewish. During a period known as the Holocaust (1933 to 1945), Hitler and the Nazi government had millions of people killed: Jewish people and anyone else they considered "inferior." Books that did not agree with their ideas were removed from libraries, bookstores, even homes — and then burned.

In 1939, German forces invaded Poland. To stop Hitler and the Nazis from taking over more countries, Britain and France declared war on Germany. Soon more nations joined the fight known as World War II.

When Germany lost the war in 1945, Jella returned to her home country. She was given the job of helping German children whose lives had been so badly disrupted. She decided that, as much as food, books were what the children needed.

A TRAVELING BOOK EXHIBIT

Believing that good children's books from around the world could create "bridges of understanding" between people, Jella wanted to set up an exhibition of such books. She was told that countries that had been at war with Germany would not send books.

Jella wrote letters anyway — to twenty countries — explaining her idea.

Nineteen countries sent books. Another sent only a letter. "Twice we have been invaded by Germans," it read. "We regret that we must refuse you."

"I beg you to reconsider," she wrote back. "We need to provide the children of Germany with a fresh start." She managed to convince Germany's former enemy that books from around the world could help children feel connected to each other, and that they were the best hope for preventing another war.

That country — Belgium — then sent a wonderful collection of books.

Among the books at the exhibition were *The Story of Ferdinand* by Munro Leaf and Robert Lawson from the United States and *Histoire de Babar* (*The Story of Babar*) by Jean de Brunhoff from France.

In 1946, Jella's exhibition of 4000 books traveled to four cities across Germany: Munich, Stuttgart, Frankfurt and Berlin. The story in this book imagines what it might have been like for children attending the exhibit at the Haus der Kunst, the art museum in Munich.

At early exhibitions, Jella saw how intensely children wished they could take a book home. She decided to translate one book into German and have 30 000 copies printed. The book she chose was *The Story of Ferdinand* by American author Munro Leaf and illustrator Robert Lawson — one of the books banned when Hitler was in power. Every child who attended the Berlin exhibit took home their very own copy of *Ferdinand der Stier*, the story about the bull who loved flowers and didn't want to fight.

International books on display at the exhibition in Munich's Haus der Kunst in 1946.

THE BOOK CASTLE

Jella longed to set up a more permanent exhibition.

Eleanor Roosevelt, the former first lady of the United States, helped convince Americans to donate money that would help Jella establish the International Youth Library. It was the first of its kind in the world. The day it opened, in a small mansion in Munich in 1949, children read from their favorite books in different languages on the radio. In 1983, the library was moved into Munich's Blutenburg Castle.

The "Book Castle" now holds the largest international collection of children's books in the world. There are 30 000 books in its lending library. In its reference library are over 600 000 titles in more than 130 different languages.

SHARING BOOKS, BUILDING BRIDGES

Jella organized a conference in 1951 that led to the formation of the International Board on Books for Young People (IBBY). Swedish author Astrid Lindgren (who wrote *Pippi Longstocking*) was also a founding member.

Jella died in 1970 at the age of 79, but her idea — that good books help children of the world understand and feel connected to one another — lives on and continues to grow. There are now more than 75 countries with their own sections of IBBY.

Since 2005, one of IBBY's most important activities has been helping children whose lives have been disrupted by war, civil disorder and natural disasters, such as earthquakes and tsunamis. Through storytelling and by creating or replacing book collections, IBBY helps the children believe in the possibility of a better future.

A portion of the proceeds from the sale of this book will go to IBBY's Children in Crisis Fund.